THE BEAUTIFUL STORIES OF LIFE

THE BEAUTIFUL STORIES OF LIFE

SIX GREEK MYTHS, RETOLD

CYNTHIA RYLANT

ILLUSTRATIONS BY CARSON ELLIS

HARCOURT

HOUGHTON MIFFLIN HARCOURT

BOSTON   NEW YORK   2009

Requests for permission to make copies of any part of the work should be submitted
online at www.harcourt.com/contact or mailed to the following address:
Permissions Department, Houghton Mifflin Harcourt Publishing Company,
6277 Sea Harbor Drive, Orlando, Florida 32887-6777.

Harcourt is an imprint of Houghton Mifflin Harcourt Publishing Company.

www.hmhbooks.com

Library of Congress Cataloging-in-Publication Data
Rylant, Cynthia.
The beautiful stories of life: six Greek myths, retold/Cynthia Rylant; illustrated by Carson Ellis.
p.   cm.
Retells the myths about Pandora, Persephone, Orpheus, Pygmalion, Narcissus, and Psyche.
I. Mythology, Greek—Juvenile literature. I. Ellis, Carson, 1975– II. Title.
BL783.R95   2009
398.20938—dc22   2007034808
ISBN 978-0-15-206184-5

Text set in RequiemText
Designed by April Ward

First edition
A C E G H F D B

Printed in Singapore

FOR HERMES
—C.R.

FOR COLIN AND HANK
—C.E.

CONTENTS

PANDORA

Z{\sc eus was ruler of the universe}, and if there were only one thing to remember about him, it was this: Never cross him. But someone did.

Zeus had always controlled fire. Men could have all the water, all the air, all the earth they wanted. But fire would remain with the gods, for it was the source of all creation. Without it, men would never find their genius, their passion, their own gods within. This was precisely what Zeus intended.

But a heroic—and some say foolhardy—man named Prometheus tricked Zeus. He stole fire from the god of gods, and as always happens in the stories of life, action creates consequences.

Prometheus not only drew the vengeance of the most powerful god in the universe upon his head. He also set in motion a story that would change the hearts of men forever.

When Zeus discovered he had been tricked by a mere mortal—a *man*—the god's anger was so searing, it might have destroyed Earth had Zeus allowed its release.

But Zeus was not only powerful. He was shrewd. He understood that true vengeance takes place quietly, intelligently, and with a plan. He swallowed his rage and made one.

Zeus took a good long look at men. He was searching for their greatest weakness, for that would be the target of his revenge.

Zeus found man's greatest weakness by first finding man's greatest strength: It was Love.

Those who get what they want—both gods and men—rarely attempt taking it outright. A blatant grab for power is not nearly as effective as a subtle one.

Prometheus, thief of fire, had a brother named Epimetheus. Epimetheus was not as cunning as his sibling. In fact, Epimetheus was naive, gullible beyond belief.

He was also lonely—but for what or whom, he did not know. There was simply a hunger in him, which had never been fulfilled.

The god of gods knew what that hunger was. It was what most men on Earth hungered for without knowing so.

What Epimetheus wanted was the love of a woman.

Up until this time in the universe, only men had lived on the earth. There were female goddesses in the heavens, but Earth was deprived of the feminine. Zeus had seen no reason to create woman. Men were both useful and uninteresting to Zeus. Why stir them up with women?

But when fire was suddenly in men's hands, and it was inevitable that they would use it to create, to grow beyond their animal natures, the question of stirring them up became moot. With fire, the stirring had begun.

Zeus loathed this situation. But he had a plan.

Zeus would create a mortal woman. He put a great deal of thought into what she would be like, and he asked the other gods and goddesses to assist in her making. Zeus invited them to contribute their best qualities to the molding of this first woman so that she would be magnificent. Naturally, they all accepted the invitation. Vanity has never been in short supply among the gods.

Aphrodite gave her beauty. Apollo gave her intelligence. Hermes gave her cleverness. And so it went, god by goddess, until finally the first mortal woman was complete and she took her first breath of life.

Her name was Pandora.

Pandora would be a gift from Zeus to Epimetheus, brother of Prometheus, thief of fire. Zeus would send Pandora with all her beauty, intelligence, cleverness, and rare femininity to Epimetheus, who was both innocent and desperate enough to accept an unearned gift from the most powerful god in the universe. Epimetheus would accept that gift in spite of the warnings from his brother, who was certain Zeus was up to something.

Pandora did not arrive empty-handed. She was delivered to Epimetheus along with a beautiful, ornate box, which came with a specific instruction from Zeus: The box was not to be opened.

Epimetheus accepted this condition without question. He did not care what was in the box. He had what he wanted and was lost in his love for her. He had Pandora.

And beautiful Pandora loved Epimetheus in return. Of course she would. She was the essence of femininity, and she instinctively gave her heart and soul to her husband. With her beauty, she pleased him. With her intelligence, she understood him. With her cleverness, she delighted him.

Pandora was everything Epimetheus had ever wanted, and he no longer hungered for anything in the world.

Pandora, as well, was deeply satisfied with her lot. She loved being a woman and wanted nothing more than to give her husband anything that might make him happy.

This is why she could not stop thinking about the box.

Surely, thought Pandora, whatever was inside the box was meant for Epimetheus, just as she was meant for him. Surely something wonderful was in there, a wedding gift from Zeus, perhaps, meant to tease them awhile until the time came to lift up the lid.

Pandora waited for word from Zeus, but it did not come. Her husband was not troubled. He was too content. Epimetheus was a man of small mind and not one to care about finding answers to mysteries.

But Pandora was made of the gods, and she cared. She cared about why things were as they were and what might be found inside a forbidden box.

Being made of the gods, Pandora was perfect in every way, perfect in all ways, except one. She lacked one quality that none of the gods ever needed and so could not have given her.

Pandora lacked patience.

Waiting for something requires a strength unknown to the gods, for they have their own magic and they concoct their own stories.

Patience is a purely human strength, sustained by hope. And if it is inspired by deep love, patience can be in its own way invincible.

Beautiful Pandora could not even imagine such a quality.

So one day she grew tired of waiting. And she opened the box.

Pandora first thought they were butterflies, the dozens of winged creatures that flew from inside. She reached for them.

Then she caught her breath. Horrified.

Each winged creature had the face
of a demon. Pandora was paralyzed
with disbelief as they flew from the
box, hovered a moment so she might
look into their empty eyes, then
disappeared through the window,
out into the world.

Pandora began to weep. She now
knew what Zeus had done. She knew
what she had done. Together they had
unleashed a multitude of sufferings
upon mankind: disease, war, starvation,
depravity, insanity. Whatever might create human anguish.

Pandora wept. But then, impulsively, as the last winged creature exited the box, this woman created of the gods reached out
her hand, caught the creature, and put it back inside.

And with that one small act, Pandora changed the fate of mankind. For what she caught and returned to the box was Hope.

Zeus had put hope in the box, along with the pestilence and the cruelty, believing that hope would not survive in a world so filled with suffering. And he knew mankind could not survive without hope.

But Pandora reached out and she captured it and did not let it go. Because she did so, and placed it back inside the box, hope is alive today. It lives in darkness.

And in darkness man finds it.

PERSEPHONE

IN WINTER, WHEN ICE COATS the thin arms of small trees and flowers die for lack of sun, Persephone can be found among the dead. She is their queen. She did not ever mean to be so, but it happened.

On the earth, Persephone had been a lovely young maiden. She had loved life, all of it: the quiet deer of the forest, the eagles in the noonday sky, the scent of rain. And Persephone had loved

best the flowers. She was herself
like a flower, soft and full of
grace. She was most at
home in a garden.

Persephone was
a mortal, but her
mother, Demeter, was
a goddess, the goddess
of growing things. It
was Demeter who fed
the world, and this pleased
her. But the true source of
Demeter's happiness was her
flower-daughter, Persephone.

It is one of the stories of life that that which is most light
often attracts that which is most dark. And so it would be for the

maiden Persephone, for one day she caught the eye of Hades.

Hades: god of the underworld. His brother Zeus ruled the sky, and his brother Poseidon ruled the sea.

Hades ruled the dead.

It was Hades who decided whether a dead man floated forever in the eternal river of regret or found peace in the green elysian fields. Though Zeus held more power in the universe of gods and men, it was Hades who always made that final call.

Hades rarely left the underworld. But one day, in search of a nightingale for his palace, he went above. Moving over the land, Hades saw Persephone walking in her gardens, and the vision of her shook him. It moved him. And he wanted her.

Soon after, on a beautiful morning among her flowers, Persephone found herself suddenly drawn toward an exquisite new bloom. As if in a spell, she moved toward the iridescent, beckoning petals.

She reached out. And in the moment of contact, the ground opened up beneath her, a massive hand reached up for her long hair, and in one terrible moment, she was gone.

As Hades sealed the opening above her head, Persephone cried out for her mother. The cry would echo for hours over the land, above the water, and up into the sky. Many would hear it, but none would respond.

Lying at Hades' feet on the cold floor of an iron chariot that carried her, Persephone felt her blood draining away, her heart slowing. Life moved out of her, and death moved in.

The underworld is neither as dark as some imagine it to be, nor as grotesque. It is, however, a place where that which is beautiful cannot bring pleasure and where anything longed for can never be found. Trees grow there, water flows. But nothing matters.

As one of the gods, Hades was himself not dead, but until

the day he saw Persephone in her gardens, he had nearly forgotten this. Hades was alive. He had feelings. And Persephone stirred them.

The god set young Persephone on a throne beside him and announced that she was now his wife and queen. Because he was who he was, Hades did not ever consider what Persephone's view of the matter might be.

As for the girl, once she understood that she was not dreaming, once she understood she was neither of the living nor of the dead, she did what she had to do: She submitted. Like a wildflower in a wind, Persephone bent herself to Hades' will, did what he asked, accepted what he offered, and became what he needed.

Hades wanted a wife and now he had one. Yet there was a part of her he would never have, the part left behind in the gardens of the earth and the flowers that grew there. The pallor of

Persephone's once-blushing skin proved it: She was a queen, but a queen without light.

MEANWHILE, IN THE WORLD ABOVE, things were unfolding.

Demeter had been told by a river nymph what had happened to her daughter. And when Demeter learned that her young daughter had died, such devastation and fury shook the earth and the heavens as they had never been shaken before. Demeter's grief was deeper and larger and louder than any mortal's grief could ever be, for she was of the gods and everything about her was both great and terrible.

The only child of Demeter had been taken. Chaos was bound to follow.

The goddess streaked a path to Zeus's throne. There, she tore at her hair and howled out her misery. She begged Zeus to get her daughter back. Only the most powerful god in the universe could overturn the girl's fate.

But Zeus refused. He reminded the goddess what she already knew: that no mortal who enters the underworld ever leaves it. It was a universal law.

And with that answer, Demeter's spirit died.

She returned to the earth, and everything began to perish.

All green things turned brown and withered. Demeter curled into herself as the decaying stems of the flowers curled into death, and all living creatures began to starve.

Zeus saw this happening and knew he must intervene.

He called for Hermes, the messenger god, and he instructed Hermes to descend to the underworld with an order to let Persephone go. Hermes was then to return the girl to her mother.

Hermes had a notorious reputation as a trickster and would rather have just stolen the girl out from under Hades' nose. But he agreed to do as he was told.

So swift Hermes descended. When he arrived at Hades' throne, he found the dark god and the pale bride sitting in silence. Hades was gazing at Persephone's face, which was now changed. Something new and deeper lay in her countenance. It was the look of experience.

Hermes announced Zeus's order and expected Hades to explode. But Hades was surprisingly agreeable. He motioned to Persephone, who then stood, placed her hand in Hermes', and followed him.

Hermes led Persephone out of the underworld. As she ascended, color returned to her face and her eyes shone. Back in her gardens, she let her fingers softly stroke the flowers as she passed by. Flowers, like the girl, coming again to life.

Persephone was delivered to her mother. But before Hermes left her, he remembered the critical question Zeus had told him to ask Persephone.

Hermes asked the girl if she had eaten anything in the

underworld, fully expecting her to say no. The pleasure of food means nothing in the underworld. She would have had no hunger, no need.

But to his astonishment, and Demeter's, Persephone answered, "Yes." Hades had offered her a pomegranate. He had told her that the gray in her face worried him. "Eat this fruit," Hades had told her. "Be well."

And holding the glistening, ruby-red pomegranate in her hands, some small part of Persephone that remembered life was awakened. Some small part of her remembered who she was.

She ate of the pomegranate. And that choice made all the difference to her fate. For anyone who partakes of food in the underworld is bound to Hades forever.

Zeus was informed of Persephone's disastrous choice, and he knew he must act and yet somehow avoid a repeat of Demeter's vengeance on the earth. He must please both the mother and the husband.

Thus, Zeus brokered a deal: He decreed that Persephone would spend a part of every year with her mother, in life, and a part of every year with her husband, in death.

And that is how it has been since. When Persephone is with Demeter, all things on the earth grow green and blossom. And when Persephone is with Hades, the earth is icy cold and draws into itself until her return.

In the underworld, Persephone is queen, and this is a role she has come to honor. Those dead who are newly arrived continue to stand before Hades, awaiting judgment. But now as they wait, these new dead look toward the face of the young queen at his side. When they do, for the last time in their journey, they connect. For only those who have loved life know what it is to lose it. Only those who have let go understand the fall.

In Persephone the dead see a mirror of themselves. And in this final communion, they rest.

ORPHEUS

THERE ARE SOME who cannot face reality. Orpheus was one of these, and the inability to accept and live the truth eventually destroyed his life.

Orpheus was a mortal, but he had a strong streak of the gods running through him, for his father was the god Apollo. Apollo was the most sensible of all the gods and revered for his ability to see to the heart of a matter. When the time came for decision making, men prayed for Apollo's guidance.

There is in this story of Orpheus a sad irony, as one day he would need his father's famous clarity and refuse to seek it.

The mother of Orpheus was not a deity, but a Muse, created to inspire. Her gifts, coupled with Apollo's love of music, produced in Orpheus a truly charmed offspring. The boy was destined to be different.

Orpheus learned to play the lyre when he was very young, and it was not long before it was clear to all just how extraordinary the boy was. For whenever Orpheus made music, all things surrendered to his spell. Fierce beasts became docile, howling winds suddenly whispered, raging oceans calmed, and all gods and mortals quieted into peace.

This is real power, the ability to control the turbulence both outside and within any man, and Orpheus had the choice to use it for good or for ill.

Fortunately, Orpheus had integrity, and he grew into a man

who valued meaning above power. He did not use his music to serve his own ego.

Orpheus eventually met and fell deeply in love with a young woman who caused his heart to surrender. Plans were laid for their marriage.

Their wedding day was beautiful. The soft winds were warm, roses bloomed, and all of the birds sang for the musician and his bride.

After the ceremony was over and the vows made, the happy couple parted to visit with their guests. Orpheus stepped away to share a goblet of nectar with his brothers as his young bride strolled through a yellow field with her sisters.

And here is where cold fate stepped in: For as she moved joyfully among the tall grasses, in her shimmering gown, filled with hope for the years to come, the bride of Orpheus was struck by a viper in the grass and died on the spot.

The anguished cries of her young husband broke even the hearts of the trees.

With any death, there always comes its sister—regret. A beloved passes from life, and there are the questions those left behind must ask—a multitude of questions that inevitably mix into just one. Could the beloved have been saved?

There has never been a truer story of life than this: No mortal can change the course of destiny.

This reality Orpheus could not accept.

Before the day was ended and his bride's body grown cold, Orpheus had made up his mind to descend to the underworld and get her back. All of his life, Orpheus had gotten what he wanted, through the magic of his music. Those who have known power are often the ones who struggle hardest against fate. They look for any way around it.

Orpheus picked up his lyre and set off for the dark caverns of

Hades. In doing so, he joined the ranks of all those sons who refused to seek their father's better wisdom before stepping into disaster.

His music opened every door. It gained him passage into the underworld, across the river of forgetting, and past the three-headed dog that guarded the gates. The music made the dog like a puppy.

Soon Orpheus was standing before the throne of Hades, sitting with calm Persephone at his side.

Orpheus played his lyre for the king and queen of the dead and sang his sad story. As he did, tears rolled down Persephone's face, and Hades himself struggled to keep his stony pose.

The last note of the song sung, Orpheus then asked the god to return his bride to him, only for a while. Just awhile, said Orpheus, time enough for a life together. She was taken so young and they had no life. Just awhile, he asked, and then the god could have her back for all eternity.

Shaken by the music, moved by the plea, and not himself at all, Hades agreed. He would allow the girl to return to the living. Orpheus, however, must obey one command: He must not look back at his bride until they had both stepped into the light above.

Orpheus agreed with all his heart. Then, from the dense gray mists, his pallid bride stepped forth, her leg still bearing the angry mark of the viper's fangs. Orpheus saw her and cried with joy.

They turned to go, she following behind, and made their way back to life, across the river of forgetting, ascending.

When at last Orpheus stepped out into the light of day, he turned around with rapture to finally embrace his bride.

But his young wife had not climbed as easily or as quickly as he. She was still just within that doorway of darkness.

"No!" cried Orpheus, reaching for her. But without even time for a farewell, she vanished. Hades would have her after all.

One death is enough for any man to bear. But two deaths were too much for Orpheus.

He lost his mind. He wandered the earth, crazed and suffering, for many months. Orpheus could not be helped.

Like a wounded animal, he was easy prey, and one day a tribe of drunken nymphs—angry that he no longer pleased them with his music—killed him. They tore him apart in a frenzy of rage and threw the pieces of him into a river.

However, with this deadly act, they unknowingly saved Orpheus from the misery of his own life. He descended for a second time into the dark regions of Hades, and his pale bride was still there, waiting.

They were at last, and for all time, together.

PYGMALION

PYGMALION WAS A COWARD. No one knew this, for he always looked so good. He was a sculptor, and his work was admired far and wide. Whenever he went into the city, young women would smile at him, linger near the fountain where he stood. Pygmalion would make a very fine husband.

Pygmalion, however, pretended not to notice the admiration.

He pretended not to care, and
to all the world, it seemed as if
Pygmalion was comfortable
simply being alone.

This was partly true.

Pygmalion, in fact, did
wish for a wife. He was
lonely. Pygmalion wanted
love and he wanted to be
loved by someone: some-
one who would bring him fruit and cheese when he was hungry
during long hours of work; someone who would smile at him and
admire his craft; someone who might lovingly apply oil to his
aching hands.

Perhaps it was not love that Pygmalion wanted so much
as notice.

But with all those girls surveying him in the marketplace, Pygmalion could most assuredly have had a wife of his own. So why did he turn a cold eye to them?

Because he was afraid.

There are many kinds of courage among men, and one of the most undervalued is the courage to relinquish control.

Pygmalion feared women because he could not control them. He had molded every aspect of his life according to his desires. He had built his own house according to his precise specifications. He ate the food he most preferred. He went to bed when he pleased, which was often in the middle of the day.

Pygmalion wanted no intrusion into his careful routine. He wanted life on his own terms, and this naturally made him a very unhappy man, with power over everything but his loneliness.

One day in the city, Pygmalion came upon the most perfect piece of ivory marble he had ever encountered. He slowly ran his fingers over it and, with his artist's touch, knew it to be in some way magical. He paid an enormous sum for it and brought it home.

Late that night, in the solitude of his studio, Pygmalion stood before the exquisite ivory marble and felt such a yearning, such an aching as he had never felt before. And without a sketch or even a clear thought in his mind of what he was about to do, Pygmalion picked up his chisel and began to work.

Pygmalion worked all night in a kind of trance, then all the next day and into the next night. He did not eat or sleep or even sit to rest his body and hands.

He chiseled and polished until he could no longer stand upright. Overcome with exhaustion, he collapsed on the floor, beside the stone, and slept for many hours. When finally he awoke, it was evening. Pygmalion opened his eyes, lifted his head, and looked up at what he had created.

It was the most beautiful woman he had ever seen.

Slowly, Pygmalion stood up and gazed at the ivory creature who gazed back at him. Her eyes were so kind.

Carefully he touched her. He ran his fingers up her smooth arm and felt something within him stir. He was entranced.

Pygmalion spent most of the following days and nights, weeks and months, in the company of the woman he had made. She was perfection. He talked to her as he worked, and told her everything: all his secrets, all his fears, all his guilt and shame and regret, all his dreams. She listened, and her eyes carried no judgment.

One day Pygmalion realized he must be in love with her. How else to explain the profound attachment? He had fallen in love with his own creation.

And it was at that moment of illumination, when Pygmalion realized his true feelings, that the goddess Aphrodite became involved.

Aphrodite, the goddess of love, was always involved when that suddenly became the story of someone's life. She watched as Pygmalion fell deeply in love with the woman he had created. She watched as his carefully controlled life fell to pieces. Pygmalion let his house become a shambles, did not care what food he ate, and went to sleep not when he chose, but when sleep chose him.

Aphrodite watched as Pygmalion let go his perfectly controlled life for love. And she was pleased.

In time, the annual feast day to the goddess arrived. Mortals journeyed to her altars to ask her favors in love. For the first time in his life, Pygmalion joined them. Having gone so deep into a life so strange, he now no longer cared what anyone might think of him, including a goddess. He needed her help.

Pygmalion went to the altar of Aphrodite and asked for only one thing: He asked her to make the woman he loved real.

That evening, Pygmalion arrived back home with a heavy heart. He had little hope his prayer might be answered, and the pain of his yearning, having been revealed, was greater than ever.

Stepping inside his dark studio, Pygmalion did what he had always done upon returning. He went to his love, to look at her and to touch her.

She was there, as always, waiting. And as always, Pygmalion bent to kiss her lovely marble hand.

When he did so, his lips suddenly warmed.

The man's heart nearly stopped beating. Pygmalion dared not believe it. He moved his fingers up the pale, smooth arm, and it was no longer hard, no longer cold.

Pygmalion then found the courage to look in her eyes. And when he did, the woman he loved looked back. She was alive.

Pygmalion married her. And because he had revealed to her

all that he was over those many months when she was but a statue, this woman—newly made but with a long memory—was more devoted to him than even Aphrodite could have imagined.

She bore him a son, a son to whom Pygmalion taught all he knew about both art and love . . . but mostly about love.

NARCISSUS

THERE ARE THOSE who fall in love with someone or something and are destroyed by the experience. This often happens because of obsession, of being consumed by a longing that is deadly to both the body and the soul. So it was with Narcissus.

Narcissus hated anything with a flaw. Yet what in life is perfect? All things possess both light and shadow. Narcissus was a perfectionist, and had he been a god, perhaps he might have created for himself the perfect experience he craved. But he was a mortal, and a deeply dissatisfied one.

Narcissus was himself a nearly perfect model of young manhood. He was beautiful, with firm-muscled arms, strong legs, clear eyes, and thick shining hair. He was so attractive that young maidens trailed after him, twirling lilies under his nose and sending whispered invitations to his ears.

They only irritated him. They were all too ordinary, and he wanted nothing to do with them. Not one could provide the pleasure Narcissus so desperately sought, the experience he so deeply craved but could never find.

One particular maiden was completely devoted to Narcissus. Her name was Echo, so named because of a curse from the goddess Hera. Hera, jealous wife of Zeus, was one day looking for her husband's whereabouts and asked the innocent maiden if she had seen the philandering god.

Echo was nervous and shy, and because she did not know where the god was, she had no answer, so she said nothing. Her silence offended Hera, and Hera cast a curse on the girl, who from that time forward could never again speak for herself, but only repeat what others said.

And it was this poor maiden who could not stop herself from following Narcissus.

"Leave me alone," Narcissus said to the girl.

"Alone," Echo answered.

"I do not want you," he said.

"Want you," Echo responded.

"I want someone more beautiful," stated the cold young man.

"Beautiful," answered Echo, with a sigh.

The hard truth about obsession is that it blinds the heart. Why would a young girl pursue a boy who so clearly held no affection for her?

Because she could not stop herself. Like a moth to flame, Echo returned again and again for the burn.

The gods were not unaware of the grandiose Narcissus. In fact, he vexed them. Who did he think he was, this mortal, seeking an experience of ecstasy? Ecstasy was reserved for the gods, and for good reason. A god could not die from a nearly unbearable pleasure. But a man could.

From Olympus, the gods watched Narcissus reject one fresh and open maiden after another, reject earthly love, and they resented his obvious sense of entitlement.

Narcissus angered the gods, and this always heralds disaster.

So it was that one day, after icily rejecting yet another ordinary girl who loved him, Narcissus walked into the forest alone. Echo followed, as she always did, hiding among the trees, longing for him.

The boy felt suddenly thirsty and all at once came upon a

startlingly clear pond. He cupped both hands and leaned over to drink. As he did, Narcissus looked into the water.

What he saw stunned him.

Looking back at him from the crystal depths was the most exquisite creature he had ever seen. Narcissus experienced this gorgeous vision, enhanced by the devious gods, and a rapture began filling him. He thought he might drown in the sensation of it as he crouched there, held in perfect satisfaction, and he did not care.

"I love you," Narcissus said to the vision that was, in fact, himself.

"Love you," Echo whispered, watching.

Narcissus gave himself to the waves of ecstasy that washed over him as he gazed at the face in the water. He did not want ever again to eat or drink, or to sleep. He cared for nothing and no one but the feelings that rushed through him to the very ends of his fingers and toes.

And in time, as obsession always does, the object of his desire drained away his life. Those things that sustain mortals—food, rest, love—no longer mattered and were no longer sought.

Narcissus could not let go, and he withered there and died.

Distraught, and as lost to insanity as Narcissus, Echo stumbled into a nearby cave, and there she wasted and died as well. To this day, anyone who enters a cave and calls her name may hear her answer.

As for Narcissus, the ordinary maidens who loved him found his body and buried him there beside the cool, clear pond. Where he lay, there grew a flower, which they then named Narcissus.

PSYCHE

IT IS POSSIBLE TO BE HEROIC without ever wielding a sword, slaying a dragon, or dying for a noble cause. While heroism always involves the fight for something, the battle can take place within oneself as commonly as it can without. The battle within is a spiritual battle and requires making a choice about what is most important in one's life. That done, then comes the challenge to protect it.

For Psyche, the choice was about love.

Psyche was the daughter of a king and very beautiful. Young men traveled to her kingdom from far and wide simply for the chance of catching a glimpse of her. There was something special about Psyche, something goddesslike. All who gazed upon her said this was so. And in their fascination with this young mortal woman, they seemed to forget the true goddess of mesmerizing beauty, the true queen of ethereal wonder.

They forgot about Aphrodite—a mistake. Jealous of the competition, capricious Aphrodite decided to destroy the girl.

Aphrodite had a son always willing to do his mother's bidding. His name was Eros, and like his mother, he was a player in the realm of love. Eros carried a sheath of arrows on his back, and whenever he had a notion to make two people fall in love, he shot a mythical arrow into their hearts and caused it to be so.

Aphrodite, who rarely liked to get messy, decided to use her son to eliminate Psyche.

The goddess instructed Eros to make Psyche fall in love with the most brutal beast he could find, one who would not love her but would instead destroy her.

Always obedient to his mother, Eros departed to fulfill his mission. He found Psyche sitting on a garden bench, but he was so stunned by her beauty that he himself loved her instantly.

Eros had not ever loved anyone.

And for the first time in his life, Eros disobeyed his mother. His arrows remained sheathed.

The young god returned to his mother's palace, and he lied, telling her that the deed had been done.

Though Eros could not bring harm to Psyche, he also could not let her go. He wanted no one else to have her. So he decided never to release an arrow into the heart of any man who looked on her. Psyche's two sisters, much less enchanting than she, found husbands. But although men still worshipped Psyche's beauty, none fell in love with her, and no one asked for her hand.

Psyche grew so lonely and wondered what could be so wrong with her that no man wanted her for his wife.

In fact, Psyche was passionately loved, though she did not know it. Eros wanted her, but he did not see a way to have her in his life. Eros was a god and she was a mortal, thus unacceptable as a bride.

And then there was his mother, who hated the girl.

Eros finally devised a plan whereby he could have Psyche without paying a price. He knew that her parents were on their way to an oracle of Apollo to ask the god what to do about their unmarried daughter. Before they reached the oracle, however, Eros himself visited the sun god. Eros told Apollo the whole story.

Apollo, a rational god, was irritated by Aphrodite's whims and agreed to help.

When Psyche's parents arrived and asked the oracle what to do about their daughter, this is what they were told:

"Your daughter is destined to wed a giant serpent, and she will be lost to you forever. Dress her in wedding garments and leave her atop the highest mountain in the kingdom. Then bid her farewell, for you will not see her again."

Utterly stricken but not once doubting Apollo's decree, the parents took Psyche to the top of a mountain and left her to her terrible fate. They kissed her good-bye and returned to their castle to grieve.

Alone, Psyche waited. Fear and sorrow so depleted her that eventually she lay down. She soon fell asleep, and when she did, a gentle wind carried her away.

When the girl awoke, she found herself lying in a field beside

a castle of sparkling stone. A soft voice in her ear told her to enter, where she would be cared for.

She did so and soon found herself seated at a sumptuous banquet, lovely music in the room, and the soft voice telling her she might have whatever her heart desired.

"Love," whispered Psyche.

"It will be yours" was the answer.

After dining, Psyche was instructed to retire to bed for the night and to leave her lamp unlit, for love would come to her only in darkness.

Psyche did so, and in the dark of night, Eros came to her. Psyche knew this was her own true love the moment she felt his touch. Eros was loving and kind, and she felt such peace in his arms. But Eros would not allow her to see him or to know his name. He told her that he would be her husband and that she would forever live in his castle, provided she never try to see him. If ever she betrayed this, he would leave her.

Psyche could not now imagine life without him. She easily agreed.

Life loves the truth. Important things that are kept in darkness will not remain there comfortably. Life will find a way to bring them out into the open: even a perfect lover who wishes to hide.

Psyche was blissfully happy in the castle, but in time she grew lonely for her two sisters. She needed to see them one last time.

One night she asked her husband if her sisters might be allowed to visit her just once, so she might let them see she was happy and alive, so she might embrace them and say good-bye.

"It is dangerous," said Eros.

"But why?" Psyche asked.

He would not explain, and at first he refused her request. But Psyche pleaded, and because he loved her so, Eros relented.

"You may see your sisters," he told her. "But do not tell them whose palace this is or anything of our life together."

Psyche agreed.

Out walking one day, Psyche's two sisters were suddenly lifted by a gentle wind, and they found themselves at the door of a castle where their long-lost sister was waiting.

The three wept with happiness. Psyche brought her sisters into her new home. Naturally, they were full of questions for the girl: Who was her husband? Where was he? What did he look like?

Unskilled at deception, Psyche tried to invent answers. She tried to protect her husband.

But her sisters were sharp. They could see the girl was lying, and they soon had her admitting that she had never, in fact, even seen her husband's face.

The sisters were also quite greedy. And in no time they were secretly devising a plan to possess the very castle in which they sat, and every sparkling treasure in it.

Psyche's sisters told her that her husband was surely the serpent that the god Apollo had decreed she would marry. It was the only logical explanation for a husband hiding in darkness. And they told her that as soon as the serpent had tired of this game he was playing, he would devour her.

Isolated, confused, Psyche could not argue with them. She began to think her sisters might be right.

They told her what to do: They instructed her to hide a knife and an oil lamp beneath her bed. While her husband slept, she would then light the lamp, expose his serpent face, and plunge the knife into his serpent heart.

Goaded by her sisters' relentless urgings, but now driven even more by her own desire for the truth, Psyche set the trap.

That evening, Eros came to her in darkness, as always. And

as always, he was loving and kind. Then he fell asleep.

Psyche found the knife, lit the lamp, and shone it on his face.

There, in the light, was the most beautiful young man. Psyche felt her heart break with tenderness and joy. He was, after all, her beloved husband.

Aching to touch him, she leaned closer. As she did, one drop of hot oil spilled from the lamp onto his shoulder.

The young man's eyes opened in pain and surprise. Then, when he saw what Psyche had done, a deeper pain crossed his face.

"You betrayed me," he said. And he flew out the door.

Seeing his wings for the first time, Psyche then knew who he was. He was the god Eros.

Devastated, Psyche fainted. When she awoke, she was no longer in the castle, but lying on rocks at the bottom of a cliff. Banished.

Psyche got to her feet. She knew she had betrayed her husband and was now suffering the consequences. Yet she loved him still. And she knew that she had two choices in this: Psyche could either fight for love or give up.

Psyche decided to fight.

She searched for Eros many days and nights but to no avail. As time passed, she fell further into despair, and she realized the gods were not going to help her.

Finally she knew what she must do. She must go directly to the goddess of love. She must seek out Aphrodite.

When at last she approached the goddess, Psyche was terribly drawn. The shock of her lover's disappearance, the unending tears, the sleepless nights: All had taken their toll.

Aphrodite gave her a haughty look.

"The 'beautiful' Psyche," said Aphrodite. "Look at you."

Psyche knelt before the goddess.

"I will do anything to bring him back," Psyche said.

"He deserves a goddess," answered Aphrodite.

"I will do anything," repeated Psyche.

Aphrodite could on occasion be generous, even kind, when the mood pleased her. But a young woman who was both beautiful and adored by Aphrodite's only son had small chance of receiving either kindness or generosity from this goddess.

Instead, Aphrodite decided to test her.

She brought forth a large sack filled with thousands of seeds of many kinds—millet, wheat, poppy, sunflower, rye, and dozens of others.

"Sort these by nightfall," she told the girl, "and you will see him."

She left Psyche alone with her task. The girl looked at the sack of seeds as tears of defeat rolled down her face. She could not possibly complete the task by nightfall. She was without hope.

This was a desperate scene. But love has its own power, and

it will draw on all of life to prevail. An army of ants suddenly appeared.

Sensing the girl's distress, they went to work, and in no time the ants had sorted those thousands of seeds. Psyche could hardly believe such a miracle.

When Aphrodite returned, the goddess was greatly vexed.

"You were lucky to succeed," said Aphrodite. "We will see how you fare with the next task." (She conveniently ignored her promise regarding the first.)

She took Psyche to a river, beside which a herd of rams grazed in a field. They were quite large and very strong, with threatening horns and shining golden fleece.

Aphrodite handed Psyche a basket.

"Fill this with the fleece of those rams," the goddess ordered, "then bring it to me."

Again she left the girl alone with her task. And again Psyche wept in despair, for she knew that not one of those powerful rams would allow her near it. She would be killed.

But again, the unexpected happened. A voice spoke to her from beside the river. It was a water reed.

"Wait until sunset," said the reed, "and the rams will go to the edges of the field to rest. Then collect bits of their fleece from the bushes against which they have rubbed themselves all day."

Psyche did as she was advised, and she returned to Aphrodite with the basket full of golden fleece.

Now the goddess was very angry.

"You think you are clever," she said. "But you will never succeed at the third task."

Aphrodite led Psyche to a raging waterfall, which was surrounded by deadly jagged rocks. She handed the girl a goblet.

"Take this goblet, fill it from the waterfall, then bring it to me."

Alone with her task, again Psyche wept. No one in the world could possibly cross those forbidding rocks to fill a goblet with water.

But just as she was about to give up all hope, life again intervened and did for her what she could not do for herself: It sent her an eagle.

And the eagle swooped down, picked up the goblet in its beak, filled it at the waterfall, and returned it to Psyche's hands.

Psyche took the goblet to Aphrodite.

The goddess by this time was beyond furious. She presented her fourth and most deadly challenge.

She handed Psyche a small box.

"Descend to the underworld, where Hades sits with his queen," said the goddess. "And tell Persephone that I wish to

borrow a bit of her beauty, for putting up with you has quite depleted me. Bring the beauty back to me in this box."

And now Psyche was truly without hope. She knew that mortals were absolutely barred from the underworld and that the three-headed dog guarding its gates would never let her pass. She would not see Eros again.

In misery, Psyche wandered down a desolate road. But though she had given up, life had not.

As Psyche passed by a tower, the tower suddenly spoke to her. It told her where to find a secret entrance to the underworld, and it also told her that if she brought a cake for the three-headed dog that guarded the gates, the dog would let her in.

Psyche did as she was told. Soon she was standing before Hades and his queen.

Psyche handed the box to Persephone, with Aphrodite's request. The queen of the underworld complied. She took away the box, then returned with it, placing it in the girl's hands. Psyche thanked her and was allowed passage back to Aphrodite.

By now Psyche had so deteriorated that she looked more like a haggard old woman than a fresh young girl. What if Eros saw her this way? In her hands was a box of beauty. Perhaps she could have just a pinch. . . .

Stopping outside Aphrodite's palace, Psyche opened the box. The moment she did, a sudden spell of sleep overcame her and she fell to the ground as if dead.

Where is love when one has given one's whole heart for it? Psyche had done all she could for love of her husband. And now she had fallen. Where was love?

In a room in his mother's palace, not far from where Psyche lay unmoving, Eros sat. He had fled to his mother when he'd left his young wife. Aphrodite had tended the burn on his shoulder and then had settled her son into a chamber to recover.

She had also locked the door.

At first Eros hadn't minded being locked in. He was relieved to have no choices, for choice means change, and Eros did not want to change. He wanted everything to stay the same. He wanted a woman who loved him but would never try to know him. Eros did not want to be known.

But he had fallen in love with Psyche, and for the first time,

Eros had desired closeness. But he had to make the rules.

Psyche had violated them.

Now Eros was locked in a room in his mother's house, facing his own formidable task: growing up. The girl he loved and who had proved her love for him again and again was within reach, if only he had the courage to stand on his own two feet.

It was time. Aphrodite had locked the door, but there is always a way out when one cares enough to seek it. For Eros, it was an open window.

Flying from the palace, he found Psyche lying on the ground. Eros wiped the sleep from her eyes and kissed her awake. Then he told her to deliver the box to his mother, for her tasks were most definitely over.

"Wait for me," he said.

Then Eros flew straight to Zeus, god of the gods, and he asked Zeus to allow a true marriage. He asked Zeus to immortalize Psyche, so Eros might bring her fully into his life.

And Zeus, who revered courage, agreed. Aphrodite then accepted what she could not change, and Psyche and Eros were married in the garden of her palace.

Psyche lived in joy ever after. She had earned this happiness through many trials and much suffering. But through it all, she never wavered in her belief that the most beautiful story of life is love.